THE
LEGENDS OF
KING ARTHUR

MERLIN, MAGIC AND DRAGONS

Published by Sweet Cherry Publishing Limited
Unit 36, Vulcan House,
Vulcan Road,
Leicester, LE5 3EF
United Kingdom

First published in the US in 2020
2020 edition

2 4 6 8 10 9 7 5 3 1

ISBN: 978-1-78226-732-4

The Legends of King Arthur:
No Ordinary Boy

Retold by Tracey Mayhew

Cover design by Mike Phillips and Margot Reverdiau
Illustrations by Mike Phillips

Lexile® code numerical measure L = Lexile® 690L

Guided Reading Level = T

www.sweetcherrypublishing.com

Printed and bound in India
I.TP002

THE LEGENDS OF KING ARTHUR

NO ORDINARY BOY

Retold by
Tracey Mayhew

Illustrated by
Mike Phillips

Sweet
Cherry

Chapter One

Merlin was no ordinary eight-year-old boy. Like a few other children in his village, he had grown up without parents. Unlike the others, his father had been a demon, and his human mother had abandoned him soon after his birth.

Being the son of a demon had given Merlin very special

powers. He could not only see into the future, but he could also make powerful potions that healed the sick, or even turned people into animals. This meant that although people needed him, they also feared him. They needed him to make their sick and wounded well again, but Merlin's power frightened them. It was the fear in the villagers' eyes that

always reminded Merlin of what he was, and of who his father had been.

Today had started like any other. Merlin walked through the small village where he lived, and where nothing ever seemed to happen. People followed him, as they did every day, asking for potions or seeking answers to their troubles.

"But can you make the nightmares go away?" an old woman asked. She panted hard as she scurried alongside him, trying to keep up.

Looking at her, Merlin slowed his pace. "Yes. Visit me tomorrow," he said. "I'll have a potion ready."

The woman nodded and began to back away, when suddenly the air was filled with the sound of thunder.

Merlin frowned. No, not thunder …

Everyone's attention was drawn to the south, curious to see the source of the noise. A few older boys shoved their way

past Merlin, almost knocking him over in their haste.

Beside him, the old woman's face twisted in fear. "What's that?" she asked.

"Horses!" someone shouted excitedly.

Quickly moving through the crowd, Merlin reached the front. His attention was fixed on the near horizon. He stared in wonder as horses and their riders surged over the hilltop, kicking up clouds of dust in their wake. Never had he seen this many horsemen. And they

weren't just horsemen—these were
knights. Their tunics bore the king's
coat of arms: a red dragon on a
golden background.

The king's men reined their horses
to a stop, leaving several villagers
coughing dust. The leader pulled
off his helmet and stood up in his

stirrups, his gaze searching the crowd before him.

"In the name of King Vortigern, we seek a boy who has no mortal father!" he called out. "A boy with great power."

Merlin's heart quickened but he didn't dare move.

One by one, the villagers began to whisper and look his way. Some even pointed in his direction. Finally, a rough hand pushed him forward, causing him to stumble from the crowd.

The leader looked down at him as the other knights removed their helmets to do the same.

"I have no mortal father," Merlin declared, lifting his chin to look directly at the knight. He didn't want to appear scared in front of everyone.

The knight dismounted, his eyes never leaving Merlin's face as he walked over to him. "And you have powers?" he asked.

Merlin held his gaze and nodded, determined to be brave despite the knight towering over him.

The knight studied Merlin for a moment, before grabbing his shirt and dragging him over to a hooded man. "Is this him?" he demanded. "Is this the boy you want?"

The man said nothing as Merlin looked up at him. He strained to see a face within the vastness of the hood.

"Well?" the knight demanded, shaking Merlin impatiently.

Slowly the hooded man nodded, making no sound. Even his horse stood silent and still, unlike the animals around him who seemed impatient to be off again and pawed at the ground restlessly.

The knight thrust Merlin toward another man, who quickly tied his wrists

together, not caring that the rope cut
deeply into his skin.

"What do you want with me?" Merlin
demanded, his fear finally getting the
better of him.

It was the hooded man who answered.

"He will ride with me," he announced, in voice that spoke of deep woods and dark caverns.

Merlin quaked, terrified at the very idea. Even from this distance, he could feel the man's power, strong and dangerous. It called to Merlin, pulling him forward even as he struggled against the iron grip on his shoulder.

Jerking him back, the second knight murmured into his ear, "It will be much easier for you if you don't try to fight us, boy."

But Merlin continued to struggle. "Where are you taking me?"

The hooded man chuckled. "You will know soon enough, Merlin."

Hearing his name, Merlin stilled. What was going on? How did this man know who he was?

Questions ran through his mind. Before he could ask any more of them, the hooded man muttered in a strange language, and Merlin's world went black.

Chapter Two

Merlin awoke to a pounding in his head and a sick feeling in his stomach. The world around him was dark and cold, and as he blinked his eyes open, he was aware of goosebumps covering his arms and legs.

He tried to sit up but his wrists were still tied together, leaving him to fall back to the ground with a cry of frustration. Slowly moving his head, he began to take in his surroundings.

A campfire had been lit in the center of a small clearing. Although the fire was dying out now, there was enough light to see the knights sleeping under their blankets. Squinting into the distance, he could just about see their horses, tethered beneath some trees.

"You're awake, then," a gruff voice murmured.

Merlin jumped. Craning his neck
he saw a knight sitting against a tree,
watching him. Shifting around to see
him better, Merlin managed to struggle
into a sitting position.

"Aren't you going to help me?" he
asked, holding up his wrists.

The knight smiled. "Why? You seem
to be doing quite well by yourself."

Merlin glared but said nothing. He
drew his knees up to his chest as his
stomach began to growl.

"Hungry?" the knight asked.

Merlin watched as the man
reached into his saddlebag, pulled
out some dried meat and tossed it to
him.

"Eat," he instructed. "You have to keep your strength up for what's ahead."

"What do you mean? What's going to happen to me?"

The knight shrugged. "You think I know?" He laughed and scratched his beard. "No one tells me anything, boy."

Merlin bit hard into the meat, still watching the knight carefully as he chewed. "You're the one who tied me up."

"You remember that, then." The knight's eyes flicked briefly across the camp. Following them, Merlin found himself looking at the hooded man sitting on a rock beyond the campfire. He was focused on the runes he had just cast, studying their symbols as they lay scattered across the ground.

Merlin swallowed hard. "Who is he? What did he do to me?"

The knight was silent for so long that Merlin began to wonder if he would answer him at all. Eventually he said, "He is King Vortigern's advisor."

"He knew my name."

"He knows many things."

"Like what?"

"That's not for me to know." The knight was studying Merlin as curiously as Merlin was studying the hooded man. "But why does he want you?"

Merlin shook his head. "I don't know."

"I don't think that's true." The knight nodded toward the hooded man. "He seemed to think you knew exactly why he was looking for you. What makes you so special, boy?"

Merlin's fear returned. A strange yet familiar feeling was creeping up on him; a sure sign he was about to have a vision. Ignoring it, he focused on the knight and said simply, "I'm different from other boys."

"Different?" the knight asked.

Merlin nodded.

"Different how?"

"I can see things sometimes—things that will happen. And I can make potions that heal the sick."

The knight raised his eyebrows. "Well then, I understand why King Vortigern wants you. A king needs someone with your … talents."

Merlin sat quietly, not quite believing that this was the real reason the king wanted him. A prickling at the nape of his neck made him turn his head. The hooded man was looking directly at him, chanting quietly to himself, preparing to cast his runes again. In that moment, Merlin had never felt more afraid of anyone.

Chapter Three

"Wake up, boy."

Merlin groaned as a hand shook him roughly awake. Opening his eyes, he blinked into the early morning light. Around him the knights were busy packing up the camp. Only the hooded man remained still, ignoring the activity around him.

"What's happening?" Merlin asked, shaking his head to clear it.

"We're moving out," the knight who'd tied his hands replied, frowning.

Merlin frowned back. "What are you looking at?"

"You had nightmares last night. Do you know you talk in your sleep?"

"What did I say?"

"You spoke of dragons. And fire."

Dragons? Merlin had heard stories of dragons from old men in the village who had seen them in their younger days, fighting for King Vortigern's father. They hadn't been seen in years, but if Merlin had seen them in his dreams then maybe … He glanced at the knight, wondering if he had heard tales too. Before he could ask, the knight was pulling Merlin to his feet.

"Come. We need to be ready to leave soon." Guiding him toward some trees, he added, "You can relieve yourself over there."

Merlin looked around, a plan already forming in his mind. "Are you going to untie me?" he asked.

Sighing, the knight pulled out his dagger, easily slicing through the rope.

Free at last, Merlin took a few steps forward before he sprinted into the trees, easily dodging low-hanging branches and leaping over tree roots.

His heart pounded as he heard shouts erupt behind him and the knights begin to give chase.

Without looking back, Merlin sprinted on. Then suddenly he froze, suspended in mid-run above the ground.

"You cannot escape me, Merlin," the hooded man announced, stepping out from behind a tree just ahead.

Merlin could feel the man's power squeezing him, holding him in place. "What are you doing to me?" he groaned, struggling against the invisible grip.

"Only what is necessary," the man replied quietly. He released his hold just as a group of knights, led by Merlin's guard, stumbled through the trees.

"Do that again, boy, and I'll see you make the rest of the journey in chains," the knight threatened, marching over to him.

Pulling him to his feet, the knight tied his wrists again, even more tightly, before grabbing his arm and leading him back to camp.

Looking back, Merlin was shocked to discover that the hooded man had vanished. "Where did he go?"

"Who?"

"The hooded man," Merlin said. "He was here."

"Don't be stupid, boy. He's in the camp waiting for you. Now that's enough. I can do without any more trouble from you."

Merlin thought better of arguing. Clearly the knight hadn't seen anything.

It wasn't long before they were back in the camp, and Merlin was seated on the hooded man's horse.

"You disappeared," he whispered. "How did you do that?"

A knight from somewhere up ahead gave the call to move off. As the hooded man flicked the reins, Merlin noticed strange markings on the man's

hands. He stared at them, taking in the unfamiliar lines and flowing shapes that disappeared beneath the man's sleeves.

"Don't stare, Merlin."

Merlin jumped at the warning and fixed his eyes determinedly ahead. Once they had left the cover of the trees to join the main road, he was fascinated to see the rolling hills of the

countryside opening up before him. He had never imagined the world beyond his village to be so beautiful, so green.

Yet for all the landscape's beauty, Merlin knew that each step was taking him closer to an unknown fate.

"How long before we reach King Vortigern's castle?" he asked anxiously.

"We will be there soon enough."

"I don't understand. Why do you need me? I'm just a boy."

"We both know that isn't true. You said so yourself to the knight: you are not like other boys."

Merlin gaped. How had he heard that from across the camp?

Sharing a saddle as they were, there was no hiding his trembling now. Merlin swallowed hard.

"Is … is that why King Vortigern wants me? For my visions and potions?"

"You have many questions, Merlin," the man said. "Soon you shall have your answers."

Chapter Four

Fire seared the night. Merlin felt it crisping his skin, but his attention was fixed on the sky above, and the flashes of white chasing the darkness. All around him were the screams of people trying to run, then the sudden, dreadful silence as they were cut down. The churning, chewing, roiling, boiling of the land as a trail of fire scored a path straight through it. Straight at him. Straight—

Merlin jerked awake, his heart pounding, his tunic soaked with sweat. He hated these visions. They never gave him the whole story, just glimpses into the future. A future he had no power to stop or change. He was often left terrified of what was to come.

Taking a deep breath, he hoped that the man sitting behind him hadn't noticed anything. Thankfully the hooded man was silent, giving Merlin the time he needed to calm down.

As his heartbeat returned to normal, Merlin realized that many hours had passed since he was last awake. The sun was setting, silhouetting the hills against a fiery sky. His breath caught again at the image. At least there was no heat. Instead, a chill breeze had begun to whisper across the open plains. Merlin shivered, wishing he had his cloak, but it was back in his village, in the hut he called home.

He sighed sadly, thinking of his home. It was only one room, with an earthen floor and a wooden roof that leaked, but he still missed it. He missed the bitter smells of his potions, the sweet smell of the lotions he made to treat burns and scrapes … He missed the woods he had spent so much time in, collecting the herbs and plants he needed to make his remedies.

The sound of knights' laughter brought Merlin's thoughts back to the present. The landscape around them had changed yet again. Rocky mountains had replaced rolling hills and open plains. Everything seemed darker now, and cold. Most of the knights had their cloaks pulled tightly around them, but the man behind Merlin didn't seem at all affected.

"How l-long now?" Merlin asked, trying and failing to keep his teeth from chattering.

"Not long."

"Is that it?" Merlin asked, pointing ahead with a finger he feared might fall off. "I-is that-t King V-Vor-Vortigern's cas-stle?" The man didn't answer, but seeing the knights' reaction, Merlin knew that it was. He smiled, glad that his journey had finally come to an end, and that he wouldn't have to ride with the hooded man any longer.

Merlin sat up a little straighter, eagerly watching the knights as they guided their horses toward the castle gates. Men and women welcomed them home, and Merlin couldn't help thinking that he'd like to be a knight. To be loved by so many, instead of feared and sometimes hated.

But they were no longer following
the knights.

"What's happening?" Merlin
demanded. "Where are we going?"

"To see King Vortigern," came the
reply.

"But shouldn't we be going to the
castle?"

"Why? King Vortigern isn't there."

"But … where is he?"

"Up there." The tattooed hand pointed to the top of an enormous mountain.

Merlin stared, taking in the sight. He had no idea how they were going to get up there. It looked too dangerous for travel.

But the man's horse seemed to have no trouble with the rocky ground under its hooves. It plodded onward, following a well-worn path up the mountain.

After a while, Merlin summoned up the courage to look back and saw the castle far below. Inside the courtyard, he could make out fires burning and shadows moving. No doubt everyone was celebrating the knights' return. He wished he was among them.

When they eventually reached the top, Merlin gasped. A huge firepit cast everything in a warm, orange glow. Rocks and tools littered the ground, and wooden carts lay abandoned as

exhausted-looking men sat around the
fire eating and talking in low voices.
To one side, equally weary cart horses
stood nibbling at what little grass or
shrubs they could find.

Most of the men stopped what they
were doing and began nudging and

whispering to each other when they caught sight of Merlin. Two knights wearing the king's coat of arms stepped forward, then didn't seem to know what to do. After eyeing Merlin curiously, one of them turned and disappeared into the darkness beyond the firelight.

"Dismount," the hooded man instructed.

Merlin did as he was told, struggling to get off the horse and landing clumsily on his feet. A moment later, and far more gracefully, the hooded man joined him.

"What is this place?" Merlin asked, as the horse was led away. He gazed around in wonder while the hooded man cut the rope at his wrists. Never had he seen anything like this before. The crumbling remains of the towers were huge, looming over him in the darkness like stone giants.

"It is my stronghold," a deep, rumbling voice declared.

Merlin turned to find a tall, broad man with a beard making his way toward him. A movement to the left drew his attention to the fact that the men who had been sitting around the fire were now kneeling, bowing their heads. Then the hooded man bowed his head also.

Merlin looked back at the bearded man, blinking rapidly. "Are you—?"

"Yes." The man smiled. "I am King Vortigern. And you are the boy I seek."

Chapter Five

"M-Merlin," he stammered, gazing up at the king. "My name is Merlin."

King Vortigern smiled. "Well Merlin, I have been waiting for you."

Merlin swallowed nervously, too scared to speak.

The king's smile widened. He placed a hand on Merlin's shoulder and guided him toward the fire. "You must be hungry." At these words Merlin's stomach growled and Vortigern laughed loudly. "Eat, boy," he offered, gesturing at what was left in the pot.

"You are going to need your strength."

Merlin was reminded of what the knight had said. "Why? What am I going to do?"

The king looked at him, shadows dancing across his face. "You mean Magan hasn't told you?" He glanced at the hooded man. Merlin shook his head. "Well, no matter. We will talk after you have eaten.

For now Magan and I must speak. Alone." He turned to the nearest knight. "Bring him to me when he's done."

Merlin watched Vortigern leave, the hooded man (or Magan, as he now knew he was called) followed behind.

Holding out a wooden bowl, a thin, bald man, with dirty clothes hanging from his body said, "You better eat, lad."

Merlin took the bowl, grateful for its warmth. Spooning some of the broth into his mouth, he groaned happily. When he was finished, he smiled as the same man offered him another bowl. He went to take it but the knight standing behind him clamped a hand on his shoulder.

"The king wants to see you."

Merlin's heart sank in disappointment.

"Can the lad not have one more bowl of food before he goes?" the man asked. "Look at him. He's nothing but skin and bone."

Merlin could have cried with relief when the knight nodded and stepped back.

"Come, lad, sit with us," the bald man offered.

Merlin did so, and his attention was soon caught up in the men's conversation. He learned that the men were slaves, brought here to build some kind of tower for the king—although none of them held much hope of it ever being completed. Every time they built more than half of it, a great rumbling in the earth caused it to collapse.

Hearing this, Merlin remembered his vision. Suddenly, things began to make sense. Putting down the bowl, he stood up abruptly and addressed the knight.

"Take me to the king," he said, ignoring the startled looks from the men around him. No one demanded to see the king.

The knight, too, stared at him for a moment before stepping back. "Follow me," he murmured, heading down the same path that the king and Magan had taken.

As they approached an enormous
tent, two guards stepped aside,
allowing them in. The king looked
around as they entered, but it
was Merlin's first look at Magan's

uncovered face that almost made him stumble. The tattoos on his hands and arms continued across his face, the shapes and patterns flowing into and around one another.

Magan's dark eyes watched Merlin carefully as he came to stand before the king.

"Ah, here he is," Vortigern declared, smiling. "Leave us," he commanded the knight, who bowed and left the tent.

Finding himself alone with the king and Magan, Merlin felt all his determination disappear and his nerves return.

"Well, boy, shall I tell you why you are here?" the king asked, taking a drink from his cup.

Merlin looked up at him. "You want to build a tower," he said.

"Indeed I do." The king stood and made his way toward the tent flap, guiding Merlin alongside him, Magan followed. Sweeping aside the flap, they stepped outside. "I want to build the strongest, most fearsome tower anyone in this land has even known," he declared, sweeping his arm out before him. "But it has proven difficult. Each time we try—"

"I know," Merlin interrupted, "I heard the men talking. I think I know what the problem is, and I think I can help."

The king smiled, but all friendliness was gone now. His hand clamped down hard on Merlin's shoulder. "I know you

can help, boy. You see, I spent so long trying to understand what was wrong, why I couldn't build here—then Magan explained it to me."

Merlin looked across to the tattooed man, who stood watching him like a hawk. Which would make him the prey, Merlin realized.

"He told me I needed the blood of a boy with no mortal father," the king continued.

Merlin swallowed nervously. "What do you mean?"

"Your father was a demon, wasn't he?" Merlin could only nod. "And he's given you power and strength beyond any normal boy, hasn't he?" Merlin tried to step back but was held in place by the king's iron grip. "It is the power and strength of your blood that I need, Merlin. Your blood will make my tower stand."

Chapter Six

Merlin stared at the king, terrified. His vision had told him what was needed, and it was not his blood. Shaking his head, Merlin managed, "No, Your Majesty, you don't understand. You don't need me." The king laughed.

"Come, lad, I know you're scared, but you have no reason to be. You should be proud to give your life for your king."

Merlin shook his head. "But you're wrong!"

The king's smile vanished. "Wrong? You dare to tell me that I'm wrong?"

"It is not blood you need, Sire," Merlin continued. "The reason you cannot build your tower is because there are two dragons living beneath a lake inside this mountain."

"Dragons? Dragons have not been seen since my father's time."

"Two are trapped under our very feet," Merlin insisted, gesturing to the ground.

The king glanced at Magan. "Do you know of this?"

Magan shook his head. "I know of no such thing, Your Majesty."

"So how do you know what my druids do not, boy?" the king demanded.

Merlin stood straighter. "As Your Majesty has already said: my father

gave me powers. I can see things, Sire. I can see things others cannot."

"And you say there are dragons under the lake?"

Merlin nodded. "I had a vision …"

Hearing these words, Magan spoke. "He did, Majesty. I saw it with my own eyes. He spoke of dragons in his sleep."

Merlin was surprised and grateful for the admission.

The king looked between Merlin and Magan before nodding. "If this is true, then I shall have the lake drained," he declared. "Magan, stay with the boy. I do not want him left alone." Turning back to Merlin, he added, "And if I find you are lying to me …"

The king left the threat unfinished, but Merlin still trembled as he watched him turn and march over to the slaves by the firepit. Hearing the king's orders, a few of the men glanced at Merlin fearfully. A memory of heat and smoke made it difficult for Merlin to look reassuring.

Looking up at Magan, he said, "When the dragons are released, they will set fire to the land."

Magan said nothing, but for the first time since meeting him, Merlin thought he saw fear in the druid's eyes.

Days passed, and Merlin was given a fine room in the castle. It seemed that King Vortigern intended to be kind, at least until he had confirmed how accurate Merlin's visions were. In the meantime, with each night of restless dreaming, Merlin's excitement grew.

Soon he would see dragons! Living, fire-breathing dragons.

But it was taking longer than he had thought to drain the lake, which gave Magan time to begin questioning his other powers. At first it made Merlin uneasy, but then he found himself answering just to pass the time.

On the seventh day the king finally announced that it was finished and gathered them outside. "So where are your dragons, boy?" he shouted up from the bottom of the cliff. He and his knights were arranged there expectantly.

Merlin and Magan stepped up to the sheer edge, peering down into the crater that marked part of the empty lake below. The other part disappeared beneath the mountain.

Merlin waited.

"Well?" the king demanded. "Where are they?"

As if in answer, the ground began to shake. It shook so violently that the king's horse reared, and his men were

thrown off their feet. People in the
nearby town dashed out of their houses
and into the streets.

From his knees, Merlin smiled
with delight. He covered his ears as a
thunderous roar filled the air. Another
soon followed as Magan dropped down
beside him.

Merlin crawled back to the edge and looked down, his eyes fixed on the dry lakebed as it began first to split, then to crumble. Suddenly it erupted, sending cracks up the side of the mountain and rocks flying through the air. A long white claw emerged, followed by an enormous, scaly head. Merlin gasped as the dragon climbed into view, shaking rubble from its wings. It was so beautiful, so majestic, with golden eyes brighter than the sun.

Screams of panic broke through Merlin's awe. The flying rocks had reached the town, and a ledge had sheared off the side of the cliff, crushing men below. The dragon lifted its head, shooting a jet of fire into the sky before

turning its attention to the people
scrambling for cover. Merlin watched
in horror as men and women were
swallowed by flames. Even at this
distance he could feel the heat on his
skin, just like in his vision.

Another explosion from deeper inside
the mountain drew his attention. A flash
of red shot from the darkness where the
lake had disappeared beneath them.
It leaped into the air, scraping a fresh
hail of debris from the rocky opening.

Gaining height, wings flapping wildly, a red dragon closed in on the white. The two clashed in midair, tails slicing the cliff face, claws tearing at each other. The white dragon snapped at the red, tearing its flesh, making it scream in agony.

The pair rolled through the sky, trailing fire in all directions, sketching jagged black shapes across the land. When they stopped, the white dragon was on the red dragon's back. Both were roaring and biting, the people below watching in both fear and wonder.

The battle was long. For most of it, it looked like the red dragon would lose. But eventually, the white dragon gave an exhausted cry and fell from the sky. It landed with a crash on the lakebed where it moved no more. Above them all, the red dragon roared once more in triumph, before sweeping its great body around and disappearing into the distance, and into legend.

Chapter Seven

Merlin gazed down at the destruction.
The white dragon, once so beautiful,
lay twisted and bloodied in the dust,
leaving a little less magic in the world.
As a creature of magic himself, it
made Merlin's heart heavy.

Behind him, Magan spoke, his voice filled with new respect. "I knew you were powerful—I sensed it many times. I just didn't know how powerful."

Merlin ignored him as the king and his men crawled out from their hiding places below. Suddenly, one of the men turned, catching sight of Merlin on the mountain. "The boy!" he cried, pointing up at him. "The boy foresaw this! He knew about the beasts!"

It wasn't long before the air was filled with excited shouts.

"Come, boy," Magan said, his voice gentle. "We must go and wait for the king."

Nodding, Merlin followed Magan back to the tent in silence, wondering what was to become of him now.

Inside the tent was warm, but Merlin could not stop shivering. His teeth chattered as he tried to warm his hands by the fire. Magan fussed about him, draping furs across his shoulders, far more respectful now that he had seen what Merlin could do.

"You will come to Avalon with me," he declared.

Avalon was the home of the druids. According to the stories, it was a place of mystery and darkness.

Merlin shook his head. "I'm not a druid. I'm not one of you."

Magan finished stirring a wooden cup and sat down across from him. "You will live among us. You will learn from us. But you shall not be one of us." He smiled. "You are something greater. Always remember that."

Merlin's heart beat faster. "But I don't—"

"You will have a home, people who understand you—people there who can help you. Your powers will grow under their guidance."

Merlin had to admit, he liked the idea of belonging somewhere, of being with people more like him. He even liked the idea of becoming more powerful.

He nodded. "I'll come with you."

Magan smiled. "Good. Now drink this," he said, offering him the cup.

Merlin took it, coughing on the bitter liquid. "Urgh, it's horrible!" he cried, thrusting the cup back at Magan.

Suddenly, the tent flap was pulled aside and the king marched in, his face stern. Merlin and Magan quickly rose to their feet.

"What was that?" he demanded. "What have I just seen?"

"You saw what is to come, Your Majesty," Merlin answered. "The white dragon represents our enemies, the Saxon invaders," he explained. "The red dragon was us."

The king gave a triumphant bark. "The white dragon died!" he exclaimed. "The red dragon killed him!"

Merlin was unsmiling. "Eventually."

"What do you mean 'eventually'?" He crossed the tent and shook Merlin by his tunic front. "Do I or do I not win the war against the Saxons?"

Just a short time ago Merlin would have been terrified by the king's anger, but since then he had seen dragons fly. If that much of his vision had come true, why not the rest?

Reaching up slowly, he removed the king's grasp. "Not you, Your Majesty," he said. "But there will come another, after you. In time there will be a boy, destined to become King of the Britons. He will be a great and noble leader. He will defeat the Saxons."

"You have seen this?" Magan asked.

"Yes."

"And his name, boy?" the king demanded. "What is his name?"

Merlin smiled. "Arthur, Your Majesty. His name is Arthur Pendragon."

CONTINUE THE QUEST WITH THE NEXT BOOK IN THE SERIES!

'This series opens the door to a treasure house of wonderful stories which have previously been available chiefly to older readers. We can only welcome it as a fabulous resource for all who love magical tales, and those who will come to love them.'

JOHN MATTHEWS

AUTHOR OF THE RED DRAGON RISING SERIES AND ARTHUR OF ALBION